King & Kayla

and the Case of the
Lost Tooth

Written by
Dori Hillestad Butler

Illustrated by
Nancy Meyers

PEACHTREE

ATLANTA

For Andy, who once wondered if the tooth fairy
would EVER get to visit our house

—D. H. B.

To my sister Lynn, who filled my childhood
with dog stories

—N. M.

Ω

Published by
PEACHTREE PUBLISHING COMPANY INC.
1700 Chattahoochee Avenue
Atlanta, Georgia 30318-2112
www.peachtree-online.com

Text © 2018 Dori Hillestad Butler
Illustrations © 2018 Nancy Meyers
First trade paperback edition published in 2018

Edited by Kathy Landwehr
Design and composition by Nicola Simmonds Carmack
The illustrations were drawn in pencil, with color added digitally.

Printed in February 2021 by Toppan Leefung Printing Limited in China
10 9 8 7 6 5 4 3 (hardcover)
10 9 8 7 6 (trade paperback)

HC ISBN: 978-1-56145-880-6
PB ISBN: 978-1-68263-018-1

Library of Congress Cataloging-in-Publication Data

Names: Butler, Dori Hillestad, author. | Meyers, Nancy, 1961– illustrator.
Title: King & Kayla and the case of the lost tooth / written by Dori Hillestad
Butler ; illustrated by Nancy Meyers.
Other titles: King and Kayla and the case of the lost tooth
Description: First Edition. | Atlanta : Peachtree Publishers, [2018] | Summary:
Kayla places her tooth in a Tooth Fairy pillow, but it disappears before the Tooth
Fairy has a chance to visit—can her dog King help Kayla find the missing tooth?
Identifiers: LCCN 2017012697 | ISBN 9781561458806
Subjects: | CYAC: Dogs—Fiction. | Teeth—Fiction. | Lost and found
possessions—Fiction. | Mystery and detective stories.
Classification: LCC PZ7.B9759 Ki 2018 | DDC [Fic]—dc23 LC record available at
https://lccn.loc.gov/2017012697

Contents

Chapter One

Waiting...

Hello! My name is King. I'm a dog.

I have a human. Her name is Kayla.

Kayla isn't home. She's at school. She's
been there for eleventy seven hours.
Maybe even eleventy seven days.

All I know is she's been gone a long,
long, LONG time.

I hear a car door slam. Maybe that's
Kayla!

I wait…and wait…and WAIT…

No one comes in.

Where is Kayla? She *is* coming home, isn't she?

What if she doesn't come home?

What if she NEVER comes home?

I hear another car door slam. Then Mason's voice: "Thanks for the ride, Mrs. Dixon."

Mrs. Dixon is Mom!

My tail starts wagging all by itself.
The door opens and HOORAY!
KAYLA AND MOM ARE
HOME!!!!

"Hi, King," Kayla says. "Guess what?
I lost a tooth today."

She opens her mouth. Her teeth smell
like turkey sandwiches. I LOVE turkey
sandwiches. They're my favorite food!

Then Kayla opens her backpack. She pulls out a small pillow. It smells like turkey sandwiches…peanut butter and jelly…pizza…apples…potato chips…cheese…

I LOVE all of that stuff!

"This is our class tooth fairy pillow,"
Kayla explains. "I put my tooth in here
so I wouldn't lose it."

That's why it smells like turkey
sandwiches! Kayla used that tooth to
eat her lunch. Before it fell out.

"The tooth fairy will take my tooth and
leave me some money," Kayla says.

"Tomorrow, I'll bring the pillow back to school for the next kid who loses a tooth. Would you like to see my tooth, King?"

"Okay," I say.

Kayla unzips the pocket. Her eyes go wide. "Oh, no!" she cries. "My tooth is gone!"

Chapter Two

Using My Nose

Kayla turns the pillow upside down and shakes it.

No tooth.

She looks inside her backpack. She
dumps everything out.

Still no tooth.

"Mom, I can't find my tooth," Kayla says.

"Where were you when you last saw it?" Mom asks.

"In the car," Kayla says. "I showed it to Mason on our way home from school."

"Then maybe you should look in the car," Mom says.

Oh boy! I LOVE the car. It's my favorite thing!

Kayla and I check the backseat of the car. I gobble up one…five…two cookie crumbs. I LOVE cookie crumbs. They're my favorite food!

We don't find Kayla's tooth.

We check the floor. I gobble up one… seven…five…six cracker crumbs. I LOVE cracker crumbs. They're my favorite food!

We still don't find Kayla's tooth.

"I wonder if Mason knows what happened to my tooth," Kayla says. "Let's go talk to him."

We wait until it's safe to cross
the street.

My nose twitches. I smell something.
It's not Kayla's tooth. It's Cat with No
Name! He's hiding under a bush.

"Hi, Cat with No Name!" I say.

"It's me, King!"

He just blinks at me.

21

Kayla starts to cross the street.

"Wait!" I tell her.

"What's the matter, King?" Kayla asks.

"Maybe Cat with No Name can help us find your tooth," I say.

He helped us find my ball once. I
didn't know he was helping because
he talked in riddles. Cats do that
sometimes. They talk
in riddles.

"Cat with No Name?" I say. "Do you know where Kayla's missing tooth is? It's not in her mouth. It's not in the class tooth fairy pillow. And it's not in our car."

Cat with No Name licks his paw. "It's wherever she left it. Now go away, Dog!"

That's not a riddle. It's not even helpful.

"Come on, King." Kayla pulls on my leash.

I should have known better than to ask a cat for help.

Chapter Three

Mason's House

We knock on Mason's door. He opens it.

"Hi, Mason!" I say.

"No lick," Kayla says.

But I have to lick Mason. He smells like turkey sandwiches and hot dogs. I LOVE turkey sandwiches and hot dogs. They're my favorite foods!

"What's up?" Mason asks Kayla.

Kayla pulls me away from Mason. "I can't find my tooth," she says. "It's not in the tooth fairy pillow. It's not in my backpack. It's not in the car. It's not anywhere!"

Wait a minute! Mason's mouth smells
like hot dogs. But his hand smells like
turkey sandwiches. Like
Kayla's teeth!

"Hey, Mason!" I say. "Why does
your hand smell like
Kayla's teeth?"

"Maybe the tooth fairy came and took your tooth when we weren't looking," Mason says to Kayla.

"She didn't leave any money," Kayla says.

"Oh," Mason says.

"Do you have some paper and a pencil?" Kayla asks. "If you want to solve a mystery, it helps to write stuff down."

Mason brings Kayla some paper and
a pencil.

"Let's make a list of everything we
know about this case," she says.

1. My tooth is not inside the tooth fairy pillow.

2. It's not inside my backpack.

3. It's not inside the car.

If I could write, I would add this to Kayla's list of things we know:

"Now let's make a list of what we *don't know* about this case," Kayla says.

1. How could a tooth disappear from inside the tooth fairy pillow?

2. Did the tooth fairy take my tooth?

3. Why didn't she leave me any money?

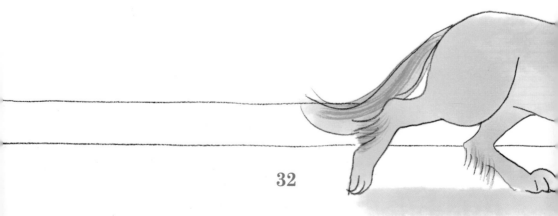

32

If I could write, I would add this to Kayla's list of things we don't know:

Why does Mason's hand smell like Kayla's teeth? Did he accidentally take Kayla's tooth and put it in his pocket?

"Now we need a *plan*," Kayla says.

I have a plan:

Search Mason!

Chapter Four

Kayla's Plan

"King!" Kayla says. "What are you doing?"

"I'm searching Mason," I say.

Mason wiggles. "Stop! That tickles!" He giggles.

Mason doesn't have Kayla's tooth.

"Sorry, Mason," Kayla says as she
pulls me away.

Maybe Kayla let Mason hold her tooth
when she showed it to him. That would
explain why his hand smells like Kayla's
teeth.

"I still think the tooth fairy took your tooth," Mason says. "Maybe she didn't leave any money because she had to quick disappear before we saw her."

"Maybe," Kayla says. "If you're right, she'll probably come back and leave some money."

Kayla and I go home. We check the class pillow. There's no money in the pocket yet.

I wonder when the tooth fairy will come back.

That night Kayla hugs the class pillow while she sleeps.

I try to stay awake. I want to meet the tooth fairy if she comes back.

My eyelids grow heavy. Soooo heavy.

I can't help it. I fall asleep.

In the morning, Kayla checks the tooth fairy pillow. There's a dollar and a note inside the pocket. There's also a liver treat! I LOVE liver treats. They're my favorite food!

Kayla reads the note out loud.

Dear Kayla,

I'm sorry your tooth is lost. If you find it, put it under your pillow and I'll come back and get it. In the meantime, here is some money for you and a treat for your dog.

—The Tooth Fairy

I LOVE that tooth fairy! She makes me feel happy…happy…HAPPY!

But Kayla isn't happy.

"The tooth fairy didn't take my tooth," Kayla says. "That means we still haven't solved this case."

Chapter Five

Found

Kayla looks at the lists she made
at Mason's house. She crosses out
something on one paper. Then she
stares at the other paper.

I stare at the tooth fairy pillow. It still smells like turkey sandwiches. The smell hasn't faded at all.

Maybe I should take another look at this pillow.

Maybe we missed something.

The pocket is unzipped.

I stick my nose inside.

Hey!

There's a hole deep inside the pocket.
Maybe Kayla's tooth went through the
hole and into the pillow.

I paw at the hole and pull out a piece
of stuffing.

Yuck! Pillow stuffing
doesn't taste good.

I paw some more.

I may have
to take this
whole thing
apart.

Look! Kayla's tooth!

"Kayla! Come quick!" I yell.

Kayla gasps when she sees the mess. "Bad dog, King!" she yells.

My tail droops. I'm not a bad dog. I'm a good dog. I found Kayla's tooth!

"Look," Mom says. She picks up the tooth.

"It must have been inside that pillow all along," Dad says.

"Yes!" I say.

Kayla takes her tooth. "King is smart," she says. "But what about the pillow? I'm supposed to bring it back to school for the next kid who loses a tooth."

My tail droops even lower. "I'm sorry," I say.

"Maybe we can buy a new one," Mom says.

Mom and Kayla go shopping. When they come home, Kayla has a brand new tooth fairy pillow.

"I'm going to put my tooth inside this pillow tonight," she says.

This time I'll stay awake. This time
I'll meet the tooth fairy...

The End

Oh, boy! I LOVE books.
They're my favorite things!

"A delightful series start that will have kids returning
to read more about Kayla and King. It's also a great
introduction to mysteries, gathering facts, and analytical
thinking for an unusually young set." —*Booklist*

"A perfect option for newly independent readers ready to
start transitioning from easy readers to beginning chapter
books." —*School Library Journal*

"Readers will connect with this charmingly misunderstood
pup (along with his exasperated howls, excited tail
wagging, and sheepish grins)." —*Kirkus Reviews*

King & Kayla and the Case of the Missing Dog Treats

HC: 978-1-56145-877-6
PB: 978-1-68263-015-0

King & Kayla and the Case of the Mysterious Mouse

HC: 978-1-56145-879-0
PB: 978-1-68263-017-4

King & Kayla and the Case of the Secret Code

HC: 978-1-56145-878-3
PB: 978-1-68263-016-7

King & Kayla and the Case of Found Fred

HC: 978-1-68263-052-5
PB: 978-1-68263-053-2